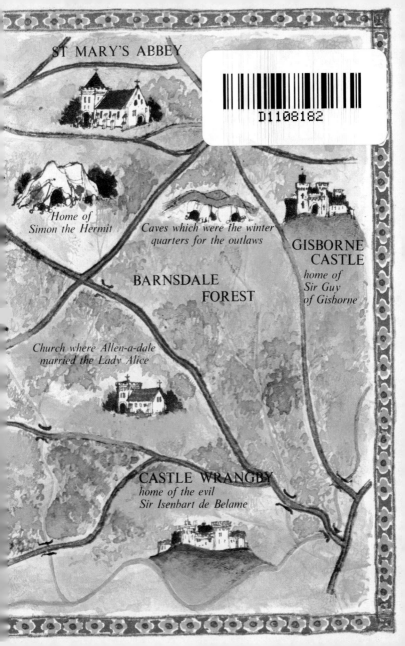

ST MARY'S ABBEY

Home of
Simon the Hermit

Caves which were the winter
quarters for the outlaws

GISBORNE
CASTLE
home of
Sir Guy
of Gisborne

BARNSDALE

FOREST

Church where Allen-a-dale
married the Lady Alice

CASTLE WRANGBY
home of the evil
Sir Isenbart de Belame

Harold, the last of the Saxon kings, died at Hastings in 1066. Duke William of Normandy, the Conqueror, became King of England. The knights and lords who had supported him were rewarded with the rich Saxon manors and estates. The Church had supported William and so the monasteries also became rich and powerful.

For many years England was ruled harshly, not only by William but by the Norman kings who came after him. The Saxon freemen as well as the villeins *(peasants)* hated the new laws and taxes and felt bitterly towards their Norman masters.

There were few books in those days. Most men could not read and so the tales they heard were sung and told to them by travelling minstrels.

The hero of many of these stories was Robin Hood. Some of the ballads which were sung about him can be read from old manuscripts though over the years the stories have been altered and added to by many writers.

ROBIN HOOD
and the
King's Ransom

by DESMOND DUNKERLEY

with illustrations by BERNARD BRETT

Ladybird Books Loughborough

Robin meets Allen-a-Dale

From the branch of the oak tree Will Scarlet could look out over the top of the forest. The ground was high here and sloped away on all sides. Three woodland paths met in the clearing below and it was these that Scarlet was watching so carefully.

'What do you see, Will?' called a voice from the ground.

'Still nothing,' replied Scarlet, 'nothing at all.'

'I think that Robin will have to eat without a guest today,' said Little John. He sank back against the tree trunk with a sigh. 'I am too hungry to wait here much longer.'

'Wait,' called Scarlet, 'perhaps we shall have

company after all.' He shaded his eyes against the bright summer sun and looked again.

Little John rose to his feet. 'Who comes, and from which way?' he asked.

'A mounted man – he looks like a knight – riding alone,' replied Will and pointed to the track from the south.

'Dinner at last,' said Little John. He strung his bow as Will Scarlet climbed down to join him.

Together they waited until the horseman entered the clearing. He was a knight as Scarlet had thought, dressed in chain mail and carrying a lance in one hand. He rode with his head down, as though his thoughts were far away. When the two outlaws stepped into his path his head came up slowly. He showed no signs of fear, almost as if he did not care what happened to him.

'Welcome to Sherwood, Sir knight,' said Little John. 'My master has been expecting you these last three hours.'

'And who is your master?' asked the knight in surprise.

'He is Robin Hood,' replied Little John, 'and he is waiting to dine with you.'

'I have heard of him,' said the knight. 'He is a good and brave man. How did he know to expect me? I would have been long past here had I felt like travelling faster.'

'Robin said that he would not dine today until he had a guest to keep him company,' explained Little John. 'We have been waiting for someone to pass by.'

'I will eat with your master,' said the knight, 'though I fear I shall be sad company.'

Twice on their way to the camp, Will Scarlet raised his hand to a figure in Lincoln green, half hidden in trees at the side of the track. After a while, they came to a wide clearing in the forest with a stream running through it at one end.

In less than one year Robin's band had increased to over fifty outlaws who were now enjoying the

sun. They stood up and gathered round as Little John led the knight's horse to where Robin sat.

'Welcome to Sherwood, Sir knight,' said Robin, moving towards him. 'Will you do us the honour of eating with us?'

'The honour will be mine, good Robin,' replied the knight, graciously. 'My name is Sir Richard of the Lee. I have heard of you often and thought well of what I have heard, so I will gladly share your feast.'

They sat down to dine on venison pie, fresh fish from the stream, new baked bread and ale. As they ate, Sir Richard told them something of his adventures. He had just returned from the Crusade. When he had finished, Robin asked, as he always did of travellers from the Holy Land, when the king was likely to return.

'That is one reason for my sadness,' replied the knight. 'When he heard reports of Prince John's bad government, the king set out for England. On the way he was taken prisoner by the Duke of Austria and is now being held by him for a ransom of 10,000 pounds.' There was a stunned silence. All the outlaws were loyal subjects of the king.

The meal was finished when Robin, who had been sitting thoughtfully, said, 'This is bad news for those who need the king back to govern England justly once again. The Lion Heart needs a ransom, so what do you say to our helping to collect it for him?' The outlaws shouted their agreement, so Robin went on. 'It has always been our custom, Sir Richard, to ask each guest who shares a meal with us to pay some toll for passing through the greenwood. From now on, until the king is free, a half of what we are given shall go towards King Richard's ransom money. You, Sir knight, shall be the first.'

Sir Richard smiled. 'I have heard, from those who wish you well, that all the money you take you use in good and kindly ways,' he said. 'This would be the noblest use of all. My sorrow is that I have only a few gold coins in my saddle bag to put towards your treasury.'

'Can this be so?' asked Robin in surprise. 'You are a knight, and hold knight's lands.'

'I am indeed a knight,' replied Sir Richard, 'but hold knight's lands only until this evening's sunset. This is the other reason for my sadness.'

Sir Richard continued his story. 'As I have told you,' he began, 'I am not long back from the Crusades. Before I took the Cross and followed King Richard to the Holy Land, the harvest was not yet gathered in. I needed money to prepare for war so I gave my Land Deed to the Abbot of St Mary's Monastery in exchange for a loan of four hundred pounds. While I was away crusading, my faithful steward was killed in ambush by men belonging to the evil Sir Guy of Gisborne.'

9

The outlaws were angry. Gisborne had caused much of their own suffering.

'Without my steward,' the knight went on, 'the harvest was not properly gathered nor the next seeding done. Now I have returned, I find I have no money with which to pay back the loan to the Abbot. The payment is due today and when your men stopped me I was on my way to ask the Abbot for more time.'

'You will not get more time,' growled Friar Tuck.

'And if you do not pay?' asked Robin.

'Then my lands and all I own are forfeit to the Abbot,' said Sir Richard, 'and he will give the deeds to Sir Guy of Gisborne.'

Robin was angry, and standing up, he said, 'There are too few noble knights left in England for us to see one ruined by Sir Guy of Gisborne and the Abbot.'

He turned to the miller's son. 'Much, go to our treasure box and count out the four hundred pounds Sir Richard needs to pay the greedy Abbot. What do you say, lads?'

'Aye!' came the cry, and Sir Richard stood up in amazement.

'I cannot accept a gift like this, Robin,' he said. 'Besides, what of the king's ransom?'

'The king would not wish to see a loyal crusading knight ill-treated like this,' replied Robin, 'and I'm sure he would approve the gift. If you wish, we'll call it a loan, to be repaid when you are able.'

'Then I accept,' said Sir Richard. 'I do not know how to thank you. The loan shall be repaid one month from today, I swear it.'

'The look of rage and disappointment on the fat Abbot's face will be thanks enough,' laughed Robin. 'In one month's time bring what you can. We will put the gold towards the king's ransom. Bring the rest in arrows, bows, swords and other things we lack here in the greenwood.'

The knight stretched out a hand to Robin. 'It shall be done, if I can find this hidden place of yours,' he said.

'We shall watch out for you,' said Robin, grasping the other's hand. 'Now go and reclaim your deed. Take Little John with you as your page. A knight should not be riding unaccompanied.' He turned to Little John. 'John,' he said, 'stay with Sir Richard while he needs you and guard him well.'

When the knight had left, riding proudly now beside his giant page, Robin turned to his men.

'Lads,' he said, 'though we are outside the laws of men, we are still within the laws of God. Today is Sunday, so those of us whose tasks are done will go to Avonlea. Friar Tuck will say a service for us in the forest church.'

Robin led twenty of his men through the forest. Suddenly Much, who was walking right behind Robin, stopped as they entered a small clearing.

'Look!' he cried, and pointed to the other side of the glade. 'An elf – a brownie! I saw one behind that bush.'

The others gathered round. Much was about to loose an arrow when Robin knocked down his arm.

'No, Much,' he said. 'The brownies, if that is what you like to call them, are my friends. They will be yours too if you show that you deserve it. Listen, all of you! Shoot at nothing in the forest which does not seek to do you harm, unless it is for food.'

The outlaws wondered what Robin had meant by this. As they walked, each looked for a sight of Much's brownie. But they saw nothing and so by the time they reached Avonlea they were laughing at Much and saying that it had been his imagination.

The little forest church stood in a clearing with a few empty huts and cottages around it. The villeins who once lived there had been moved by their lord to his larger estate a little way off. The church had no regular priest and was used as a place of rest and prayer by tired travellers.

Although the day was warm and sunny it was dim and cool inside the little church. What little light there was entered through narrow windows in the walls. The only person in the church was a young man dressed in the light chain mail and surcoat of a squire. He lifted his head and watched as the outlaws filed in. Robin liked the look of this young squire.

Friar Tuck was halfway through the service when he stopped as the church doors creaked open. The kneeling outlaws turned at the sound. They watched with fear and amazement as a small figure no larger than a boy, and yet a man, crept past them along the aisle.

The tiny dark-faced figure, dressed in a smock of deer's skin, made his way as softly as a hunting cat to the front of the church. He whispered a few words to Robin, received a reply, and crept out again as silently as he had entered. The outlaws nudged each other. Much smiled in triumph as the little man passed by!

Friar Tuck realised that something was amiss. He brought the service quickly to a close and Robin stood up, and looked round at the outlaws, his face stern.

'Men,' he said, 'we have been followed. Our enemies are too close now, so we must make a stand and fight them off. Will! Bar the doors. Tuck! Take Much and see the back way is secure. The rest of you to the window slits. Do not shoot until I give the word and then make every arrow count.'

While these commands were being obeyed, the squire came up to Robin.

'Who are these enemies, sir, who seek your lives?' he asked.

'Niger le Ravener, one of the knights of Castle Wrangby, together with a score of men-at-arms,' replied Robin grimly.

'Castle Wrangby – the "Evil Hold"!' exclaimed the squire fiercely. 'Then I will help you, if I may. The Lord of Wrangby, Isenbart de Belame, is my most bitter enemy.'

'Then join us,' Robin said, 'and we will talk again when this is done.'

'They come, master!' came a cry from a young outlaw guarding one of the windows. 'See, they have gathered on the far side of the clearing!'

'Notch your arrows,' called Robin. He took position at one of the arrow slits. 'Mark your man, but wait until I give the word.'

Fifty yards away across the grass, the unmounted men-at-arms were being jostled into line by a knight on horseback. His shield bore a black raven crest.

'Niger le Ravener,' said Robin. 'Steady, lads. They come.' The soldiers were only twenty paces away when Robin called 'Shoot!' At that short distance even the least skilful bowmen among the outlaws could not miss. Eight of the men-at-arms fell, pierced by one or more arrows. Several others stumbled with arrows in their shoulders or legs, and made off into the trees as best they could. The knight's horse fell too but the rider was thrown clear and he stood, waving his sword and

raging at his men to stand firm. A few obeyed but these also fled when the church doors were opened and Robin, with the young squire, led his men out.

'Le Ravener is mine!' cried the young man, making for the Norman. Although he was cruel, he now stood bravely alone. The fight between the two was fast and furious but the knight in heavy armour was no match for his vengeful young opponent. The duel was soon over.

Robin called back his men who had been pursuing the fleeing soldiers. He stood looking down at the body of Niger le Ravener.

'It was well done, for he deserved to die,' he said. 'But tell me, who are you and how do you come to hate the Lords of Wrangby?'

'My name is Allen of Skelmersdale, squire to my father, Sir William of Skelmersdale,' he replied. 'Men call me Allen-a-Dale. I love a maiden, the Lady Alice of Beaulieu. Belame owns her father's manor and in two days' time will force her to marry a rich, old knight as evil as himself. This is the reason for my hatred, and it was despair that brought me here.'

'Reason enough for hatred,' said Robin, 'but not for despair. I am Robin Hood, and there may be something we can do in this. First we must move to the safety of the greenwood. The rogues who fled will tell what has happened here and then we shall have a hornet's nest about our ears.'

Late that evening, around the camp fires, a plan was made. Will Stutely, who knew the forest ways almost as well as Robin, was sent to Beaulieu with a message for the Lady Alice.

Then Much turned to Robin and said, 'What of

my brownie then, master? Did I not see him in the forest after all, before he brought the message into church?'

'It was no elf or brownie that you saw, Much. So that none of you will think that in the future, it's best you see him again now to rid you of your fears and superstitions. Tull! Show yourself, little one.'

The outlaws started back in terror. A small dark figure rose, as if by magic, from a shadowy patch of bracken at Robin's side.

'This is Tull,' said Robin. 'It was his brother, Caw, who brought me the message. He is now watching the ways from Castle Wrangby. They are my true friends. Many times they have helped me and saved my life.'

The little man said nothing. His black eyes glistened in the glow of the fire as he looked at Robin.

'How did you come by such friends?' asked Friar Tuck, looking at Tull in wonder.

'By chance I was at hand to save them from superstitious cowards who thought that they were evil spirits of the woods. These people sought to smoke them out from the grassy mounds in which they live,' replied Robin. 'Though that debt has more than been repaid, they still guard me. I have no comrades who are more loyal. Now they will be your friends,' he added, 'for we are all of the forest.'

Tull looked at each of the outlaws in turn. Then he raised his hand in salute and with a last look at Robin, the little man faded into the darkness of the trees.

The Wedding of Allen-a-Dale

'Don't stand there gaping at your betters, Jack,' said Ket the smith sternly to his young helper. 'I shall need wood for the forge before nightfall, so you had best go now and gather some.'

'Yes, I will, right away,' replied Jack. He was still watching the little cavalcade of riders as it approached the smithy. 'It grieves me, though, to see my lady's face so sad.'

The big blacksmith looked up from the horse's shoe he was shaping. The lord of the manor, Sir William of Beaulieu, rode in front of the group. His face was grave as he talked to his steward who rode beside him. The Lady Alice looked pale and sad. She followed her father with an attendant at her side. Last came two young squires, riding in silence and holding slack reins.

'She has reason enough to look sad, poor lass,' growled Ket. He struck the anvil an angry blow. 'There is nothing we can do about it. Go to the forest for the wood I need before the lord sees you idling!'

The young man was about to obey when the riders stopped at the forge. Ket and Jack both bowed their heads to their master.

Many years ago an ancestor of Sir William's had fought for the Conqueror at Hastings. He had been given the Saxon manor of Beaulieu as reward. It had been his then to hold for the king, but over the years, changing times and fortunes had seen it taken into the vast Wrangby estates. Now Sir William was a tenant of Sir Isenbart de Belame, Lord of Wrangby.

Unlike Belame however Sir William was a firm but just lord. The estate was well run and as long as the rents were paid, and the tithes and taxes delivered, Beaulieu would remain his. This was written on the great Land Scroll held by the king himself. Nevertheless in these changing times, with the king away in the Holy Land, there were ways in which a lord as rich and as powerful as Isenbart de Belame could force his will upon those less powerful. Now Belame was using all kinds of threats to force Sir William to wed his daughter to old Sir Ralph de Greasby.

While Sir William spoke to his blacksmith, Jack watched the Lady Alice. Jack's widowed mother had been her nurse and he and Alice had been playmates when they were young. When his mother died, he had gone to live with Ket the blacksmith to learn the trade. He had hardly seen the Lady Alice at all since then. Lately however she had remembered him from their childhood days because she needed someone she could trust. Alice had given him messages to take to her sweetheart, Allen of Skelmersdale. Jack was terrified of the dark tracks through the forest but he undertook these errands bravely. He would willingly have died for the Lady Alice, had she demanded it of him.

He watched her now, waiting and hoping for a sign that he could be of help. Her eyes, wet with tears, remained downcast. She only gave Jack one sad look as she rode off with her father. Heavy of heart, Jack took the woodcart and made off across the common land to the forest's edge. The best wood for charcoal grew there.

He struck each blow of his axe at the imaginary heart of Isenbart de Belame, the cause of all Beaulieu's misery. Though Jack had only seen Belame once, he would never forget the cruel, hawk-like face of the Wrangby lord. Jack was so angry and worked so hard that he did not hear the stranger approach. When a voice spoke to him from the trees, Jack swung round in alarm and fear with his axe raised to defend himself.

'I mean you no harm,' said the stranger.

Jack looked at the tall figure who stood before him. The tunic and hose of green were well worn and torn in places. He carried a long bow of yew wood, arrows were in his belt and a sword hung at his side. The bearded face seemed honest enough though, and Jack slowly lowered his axe.

'What do you want?' he asked.

'I seek Jack, the apprentice to Ket the Smith of Beaulieu,' replied the stranger.

Jack was startled to hear his own name and again took a firmer grip on his axe.

'Why do you want him?' he said.

'I will tell Jack and no other,' replied the stranger. 'If you know this Jack and where he is, go tell him that I await him here. Tell him also that I showed you this.'

At the sight of the gold ring, Jack gave a cry of rage and swung his axe high as if to strike.

'Hold!' laughed the stranger, backing away. 'So you are Jack. Allen-a-Dale told me you would know the ring. He did not warn me you would go berserk at the sight of it!'

'How did you get the ring?' demanded Jack roughly. 'I do not know who you are but if you have harmed the squire I'll . . .'

'Peace, lad,' said the forest man. 'Allen-a-Dale sent the ring and asks you to take it to the Lady Alice with a message, as you have done before.'

'The time for sweet messages is passed,' growled Jack. 'Tomorrow she is being made to marry an old knight called Greasby. He is fat and evil and cruel, but he is a friend of the Lord Belame and so it must be done.'

'We know this, Jack,' said the other quietly, 'so take the ring and give the lady this message. Say to her, "Do not despair for help is at hand."'

'Help!' said Jack. 'Who can help my lady against the power of Wrangby? What can you and young master Allen do against so many?'

'Then say this also,' said the man in green, patiently. 'Tell the lady that, as well as from Allen, the message comes from Robin Hood.'

'Robin Hood!' exclaimed Jack. 'Are you an outlaw then? One of Robin Hood's men?'

'I am, and proud to be so,' replied the other. 'Will Stutely is my name.'

Jack looked at the outlaw in admiration. 'The same Will Stutely that the travelling storyteller spoke of when he passed through here two nights back?' he asked. 'The one who went to Nottingham Castle in disguise and . . .'

'I had a part in that,' Will interrupted with a laugh. 'But go now. Deliver the message to the lady, and say nothing to anyone.'

With a last excited look, Jack took the ring from the outlaw's hand and set off. Will Stutely called him back.

'The cart, Jack,' he reminded him. 'If you leave it here unattended it will seem strange and questions will be asked.'

Jack ran back. He seized the cart handle and turned to say farewell but there was no sign of Will Stutely. The forest looked as still and empty as it always did.

Next day dawned with bright sunshine and the villagers of Beaulieu began to gather early in front of the little church. Suddenly there was the sound of horses' hooves along the road from the north. Twenty men-at-arms clattered into the square and rode roughly through the startled villagers. The soldiers scattered them and took up their positions on either side of the church door. They were fierce looking men and wore the crest of Sir Ralph de Greasby, Lord of Hagley Fen.

The frightened villeins huddled in groups as the horsemen stared at them in scorn.

'Is it from rogues such as these that our lord fears a rescue?' called one with a coarse laugh.

'Keep silence!' roared the one who seemed to be their leader. 'Or we shall see if you like the whipping post when we return.'

There was a sullen silence, broken only by the horses as they stamped their feet or snorted and tossed their heads. Then the soldiers sat upright in their saddles and straightened their lines as two knights and a squire entered the square.

Sir Ralph de Greasby was old and grey, with an ugly red face. His lips were thin and the small fierce eyes had seen much cruelty. Beside him rode his nephew, Sir Hugh of Hagley who, though much younger than his uncle, was already well known for his evil ways.

'Has the lady arrived yet?' Greasby called in a high pitched voice.

'Not yet, my lord,' replied the leader of the men-at-arms.

'This is the last time she will keep me waiting,' said the old knight with a thin laugh. 'What say you, Hugh?'

'I do not doubt that you have ways to keep her strict to time in future,' his nephew replied.

'Perhaps a song would help to pass the time of waiting, noble lords,' said a voice.

'Who dares to speak before being spoken to?' snarled Sir Hugh. He swung round and raised a mailed fist.

'Just a poor minstrel, lord,' replied the man. He backed away from the haughty Norman and held his harp as though to protect it from harm.

'Well, be gone rogue, before I give you something to sing about,' said Sir Hugh raising his fist again.

'Wait, nephew,' put in Sir Ralph, holding back the other's arm. 'We need music at a wedding, even from such a rascal as this.' He looked down at the minstrel with distaste. 'Get inside the church and when my lady comes, play something cheerful or you will answer for it,' he said.

'I will, my lord, I will,' said the minstrel. He bowed his head and hurried off. He stumbled over the long gown he wore and almost fell.

'Let the fool through,' called Greasby to the soldiers who were guarding the doors.

The minstrel gathered his robe about him and disappeared inside the church. Sir Hugh touched his uncle's arm.

'The lady comes prepared, uncle,' he said. 'She even brings her own priest with her.'

Sir William rode slowly into the square, his daughter beside him. A burly friar walked at her horse's head holding the bridle. There were murmurs of pity from the villagers when they saw her sweet young face.

'See how calm she looks,' whispered one.

'Aye, the time for tears is passed and now she knows it has to be,' replied another.

The Lady Alice held her father's arm and did not glance at Greasby as she followed the friar into the church. Sir Ralph, a crafty smile on his face, went in also, with Sir Hugh at his side. A few of the villeins managed to creep in and sat down at the back before the men-at-arms closed the oak doors.

The minstrel's harp played softly as Sir William and his daughter walked slowly down the aisle and stood in front of the waiting priest. He raised his hand and the music and the murmuring stopped.

Then in a loud voice that filled the tiny church, the friar called out, 'This wedding must not go on! It has been forced upon the lady and so is not fitting in the sight of God!'

There was a moment's stunned silence. Then Sir Ralph rasped his sword from its scabbard and took a step forward.

'What is this?' he cried in furious disbelief. 'You miserable rogue!' Turning to the priest he raged, 'Perform the service now or, priest though you be, I'll have your head. Do it, I say!'

'And I say no!' said a voice from the shadows. The minstrel stepped forward. His robe had gone and he was dressed now in Lincoln green. Gone was the harp and in its place a sword pointing at Greasby's heart.

Sir Ralph was so furious he could scarcely speak. 'Who are you, knave? How dare you stand against me?' he raged.

'I am Robin Hood,' replied the tall figure in green. He blew a loud note on his horn.

Sir Ralph flung himself at Robin and the church echoed to the first clash of swords. 'The door, Tuck!' cried Robin. The men-at-arms had recovered from their surprise and were starting down the aisle to help their master. Friar Tuck seized a long bench from the front of the church and with a great heave, flung it in the faces of the soldiers. They fell, cursing and reeling. Friar Tuck drew a sword from under his gown and fought his way through to the doors. He flung them open and turned to face those of the men-at-arms who were still standing.

In the square outside, many of the onlookers had thrown off their country smocks. Now over twenty figures in green, led by Allen-a-Dale with Little John, attacked the guards outside the church. When the doors opened behind them, these soldiers were pressed back. Soon the church was full of fighting men.

Sir Ralph was no match for Robin who quickly killed the evil knight with a thrust to the heart. Robin turned to face Sir Hugh. He had taken advantage of the confusion and had left his uncle to defend himself as best he could. Sir Hugh dashed to where Sir William stood shielding his daughter. He knocked the older man to the ground with a single vicious blow and swept the Lady Alice from her feet. Sir Hugh carried her, struggling furiously, out of the small side door. He flung her into the saddle of one of the waiting horses and, mounting behind her, spurred forward through the crowd.

Suddenly a figure sprang up on the horse's back behind the knight. Before Sir Hugh could turn he saw the flash of a knife blade and felt an instant's blinding pain in his chest. He swayed in the saddle and then fell from his horse. Jack, apprentice to Ket the smith, seized the reins and brought the frightened horse to a standstill.

There was a wedding after all, that day at Beaulieu. When it was over, Allen-a-Dale took his bride back to Sherwood. With them went a new recruit to the outlaw band. A young black-smith, who wore on his finger a ring of gold given to him by Allen-a-Dale.

An Unexpected Guest

Little John had returned from service to Sir Richard of the Lee. He was kneeling down putting a small bag of coins into an oak chest.

'There, that's the last of it,' he said. The big outlaw stretched up and rubbed his back. 'I am too tall to bend down for so long,' he groaned.

Allen-a-Dale checked the total.

'What is the count, Allen?' asked Robin Hood.

'Close on four hundred pounds,' was the reply. 'Another hundred and this chest can go to London like the first.'

'Four hundred pounds?' said Little John. 'That's the same amount we gave Sir Richard of the Lee to pay back the Abbot.'

'Not gave,' said Robin. 'If you recall, it was a loan, to be repaid in gold or goods.

'The loan was made one month ago today, so perhaps we will fill this chest by nightfall after all. I don't doubt that Sir Richard will keep his word.'

'Aye, he is an honest man,' agreed Little John. Then he laughed. 'I'll not forget the time the knight put down the bag of gold and demanded back his Land Deed. I thought the Abbot's fat red face would burst with rage and disappointment. He had been so sure Sir Richard would not come.'

'And we are just as sure he will,' said Robin. 'He will not find us without help, so post men on the southern road to watch for him, John. Also lookouts at Holmlea Oak where the four tracks meet. Perhaps there will be travellers passing whose purses will help to fill this chest if Sir Richard does not bring enough gold to do it.'

Little John left to carry out his instructions. Allen-a-Dale and Friar Tuck helped Robin to stow the treasury box away safely in a hidden cave.

Sir Richard of the Lee had told them of the king's captivity and of the tax that was being levied by the Lord Chancellor in every county in England to raise the ransom. Since then, Robin and his men had been collecting money. They were loyal subjects of King Richard and longed for him to return home. All the fine clothes and armour in their store had been sold. This money, together with half of the gold in their treasury, had been packed into a chest and then been sent to the Mayor of London under a strong guard, with a note which said, 'From Robin Hood and the freemen of Sherwood Forest, for the King's speedy return.'

Half of everything that was collected in toll from the rich travellers passing through the forest was put into the second chest. If some rich merchant, knight or miserly abbot seemed to grudge the king his freedom and was trying to avoid paying the Chancellor's tax, then Robin and some of his men would pay a visit and do the tax-collector's job for him. In these ways the chest had become nearly full.

Robin was so sure that Sir Richard would come that the morning was spent preparing a feast in his honour.

'We will also prove to our friend,' said Robin, 'that the best bowmen in all England live here in Sherwood. See to the stringing of your bows and choose your straightest arrows. When we have eaten, we will put on an archery contest.'

While the cooks baked bread and prepared fish and venison, the best archers among the outlaws prepared their weapons. Robin, meanwhile, devised the target at which they would shoot.

The sun was already high overhead by the time these preparations were all complete. Robin and his men were resting when one of the scouts who had been posted at Holmlea Oak came running in.

'Four monks approaching the crossroads from the north,' he panted.

'Take your time and get your breath, lad,' laughed Robin. 'Now, are they travelling friars, or is there more to tell?'

'They are well mounted, Robin,' said the scout, 'and too richly gowned for ordinary monks. An abbot at least, as far as Dodd and I could see.'

'Let's go and take a closer look,' said Robin. He left most of the men in camp to make Sir Richard welcome and set out with Little John, Will Scarlet and Allen-a-Dale.

The Abbot reined in his horse sharply as a tall figure in green stepped onto the track in front of him.

'Hold, Sir Abbot,' said Robin Hood, 'there is a toll to be paid by those who pass through Sherwood.'

'Toll?' said the Abbot in surprise. He looked at the outlaw from beneath the deep hood of his cloak. 'I know of no toll for riding the king's highway. Who are you?'

Robin gave a bird call through cupped hands and his companions came from the bushes to join him on the path.

'We are freemen of Sherwood,' replied Robin. 'We live on the king's deer and whatever rich travellers will give us. As to its being the king's highway,' he went on, 'it is, and we hold it safe for his majesty until he is home again. Before that can be, my lord Abbot, as you have no doubt heard, the king needs ransoming. Only half of what you give us is for our needs, the rest is for King Richard.'

'Good forester,' replied the Abbot, 'although the cause you speak of is a worthy one, I wonder, nevertheless, who you are to set yourself up as lord of Sherwood Forest.'

'I am Robin Hood,' replied the outlaw leader. 'I was driven to live in the greenwood by the cruel and greedy lords that the king left to govern England. But we love King Richard and so we collect money for his ransom.'

'I regret that we only have forty pounds, Robin Hood,' said the Abbot, 'but we will give you that.' He handed Robin a leather purse.

Robin took the purse and counted out some of the coins. 'When an abbot speaks like an honest man we do not search his saddle bags to see if what he says is true. You sound like a loyal subject of his majesty so I give you back half of your money. We will only keep the half that is King Richard's share. Now, fare thee well.'

Robin stood aside to let the Abbot and his companions ride on, but the hooded figure spoke again.

'One of the tales told of Robin Hood is that he does not let a hungry man pass by,' he said. 'We have been travelling since dawn and having learnt your name, we hope the tale is true.'

'It is,' said Robin with a laugh, 'and I ask your pardon for my lack of hospitality. Will Scarlet, speed ahead of us and warn the cooks to expect company.' Then he turned to the Abbot. 'I trust that you won't object to a dinner of royal venison?'

'Not at all,' replied the Abbot, 'and I'm sure the king would not mind, if he were here and as hungry as I am.'

While they were eating, the Abbot asked again about the things of which Robin had spoken earlier.

'I am surprised you have not heard of the evil ways of Prince John and his friends,' said Robin. 'Though the Prince is King Richard's brother, he bears no love for the king's Saxon subjects.'

'I have been away a long time,' the Abbot said. His voice was so sad and serious that Robin looked keenly into the shadowed face beneath the hood. He could not see his guest's features, however, for the Abbot turned his head away before speaking again.

'Is it only the king's Saxon subjects that are badly treated?' he asked.

'No,' answered Robin. 'Anyone who stands for truth and justice, be they Norman or Saxon, must now look to their lives and property.' He told them of Sir William of Beaulieu, Sir William de Beauforest and Sir Richard of the Lee.

'Sir Richard of the Lee?' said the Abbot in surprise. 'Was he not crusading with the king?'

'He was,' replied Robin, 'but he returned a month ago to find his lands forfeit to the Abbot of St Mary's and Sir Guy of Gisborne. We lent the good knight money from our treasury so he could reclaim his land. We expect him here today to pay back what he borrowed.'

'The knight is coming here today?' asked the Abbot.

Robin waved a hand at the archery targets which had been set up. 'These preparations are in his honour. While we wait for him perhaps you would care to see how we pass our time here in the greenwood.'

'I would,' said the Abbot. 'I have heard tales of your marksmanship which are hard to believe.'

A few outlaws were chosen to shoot at different kinds of marks of increasing length and difficulty. Their shooting was so accurate that on several occasions the Abbot turned and spoke to his companions.

'This is marvellous shooting, Master Robin,' he called. 'It surpasses even the tales that are told!'

'The last and hardest test is still to come,' said Robin with a laugh. He helped Little John to set up the target. The Abbot was heard to say to his companions, 'No archer in the world can hit that mark unless it be a lucky shot. I'm sure Scarlet will have no need to renew *that* target!'

The mark was a willow stick as high as a cloth-yard arrow and the width of a man's finger. It was set one hundred paces away. To make it even harder, the outlaws had to send their arrows through a loop of beech leaves no wider than a hand's span. This was fixed above the ground, at the height of Little John's head, midway between the marksman and the tiny stick of willow.

The Abbot and his friends leant forward as the four outlaws who had passed the earlier tests stepped forward to try this last trial of their skill. Each was to shoot three arrows which they were now selecting with great care. The reward for failure was to be a blow with a heavy sack of grain wielded by Friar Tuck!

There was a great cheer as Little John's first arrow hummed through the circle of leaves and split the willow. Scarlet replaced the broken stick and there was another roar as the second arrow also hit the mark.

'By Heaven!' exclaimed the Abbot. 'This is no lucky shooting.'

The cheers turned to shouts as Little John's third shot missed the leafy circle. Friar Tuck knocked him to the ground with a mighty blow.

Will Stutely suffered the same fate when the third of his arrows also missed the mark. Poor Dodd of Lincoln had to pick himself up twice from the grass.

Then Robin stepped forward and the loud cheers rang out as his first two arrows split the willow. The noise of the cheers was nothing to the great shout that went up as Robin's third arrow sped through the circle only to bury itself in the turf, two inches away from the willow stick.

'A miss!' they cried. 'The forfeit!' Robin smiled ruefully as Friar Tuck stepped forward with the grain bag. As Robin was expecting the blow, the friar handed the bag to the Abbot.

'Would you perform the honour?' he said with a smile.

Before the Abbot could reply there was a commotion at the far end of the clearing.

Sir Richard of the Lee rode in with his attendants and the scouts who had been sent to watch for him. Robin started forward to welcome the new visitor but there were cries from the outlaws.

'The forfeit first! The forfeit must be paid!'

'I had thought I would escape it,' Robin laughed. 'Strike well, Sir Abbot, for I did miss the mark.'

The Abbot had drawn the monk's hood closer around his head upon the arrival of Sir Richard. He seemed reluctant, but the shouts of the outlaws were so insistent that he took the bag from Friar Tuck. He rolled back his sleeve and struck a blow that knocked Robin clear off his feet. The force of the swing made the Abbot's hood fall back from his head. It revealed a bronzed and noble face. The outlaws' shouts turned to cries of amazement and then to silence. At the sight of the Abbot's face Sir Richard leapt from his horse and ran towards the Abbot crying, 'It is the king! Kneel, Robin, kneel!'

The Abbot threw back his long black gown to show beneath it a rich silk robe embroidered in gold with the royal arms and crests of England.

Robin Hood and his men bared their heads and knelt before King Richard the Lion Heart.

'I have been found out,' said the king with a laugh. 'Why do you kneel, Robin? Have I not heard that you are King of Sherwood?'

'Most noble lord and king,' replied Robin Hood humbly, 'we are your majesty's most loyal subjects and crave your pardon for . . .'

'Let us not talk of pardons,' the king said. 'That was given when we first spoke and I could see your loyalty. It is for me to give you thanks, Robin, for all the tax collecting you have done to get me freed and home so quickly. I came in disguise to meet the man who, though an outlaw, seemed from what I heard to be more loyal than many in high places. I thank you, Robin Hood, with all my heart, and ask you for one further service.'

'Your wish is my command, sire,' said Robin.

The king turned to his companions who now stood in the armour and red-crossed surcoats of crusading knights.

'These are three of my most valiant lords,' he said to Robin. 'Sir William de Crouch, Sir Gerald de Boismaison and Sir Geoffrey de Broom. When you were shooting at those marks we all agreed that if we took you all back to the Holy Land with us, Jerusalem would be ours within a month.'

'Sire,' began Robin but King Richard held up his hand.

'Hear me out,' he said. 'I have since thought more about it. My lords and I now feel that you can best serve England and your king by staying here in Sherwood to continue fighting cruelty and injustice. Our meeting must remain a secret, though, until I return again. Then you and I, Robin, will put to right the wrongs that England suffers. What do you say?'

Robin Hood drew his sword and raised it high above his head.

'God save King Richard!' he called. All the outlaws answered with a shout which rang far and wide through Sherwood Forest.

SHERWOOD FOREST

This picture has been based on a map of Nottingham and the Sherwood forest area. It shows where some of the events in the stories may have taken place and where some of the places mentioned in the books might have been situated.

LOCKSLEY HAL

where Robin lived before it was burn down and he beca an outlaw

COPMANHU

Robin Hood me Friar Tuck

Log over the stre where Little John fought Robin Ho

Mounds which were home of Tull and Ca

Main summer quarters fo Robin Hood and his men

OUTWOODS HUNTING LODGE

NOTTINGHAM CASTLE
home of the Sheriff of Nottingham

to ASHBY